POKÉMON®
DIAMOND AND PEARL ADVENTURE!

vizkids
POKÉMON
DIAMOND AND PEARL ADVENTURE!
1

Coming Next Volume

Clearing each game with just moments to spare, Sanshiro meets other contestants who aren't very happy that he's succeeding. Mick will do anything to get ahead—lie, cheat or steal. And he's out to take advantage of Sanshiro's trusting personality...

Coming May 2009!

Backwards Game

BAKÉGYAMON

VOL. 1

MITSUHISA TAMURA

Contents

1

CHILDREN WITH DREAMS OF ALL KINDS!
RUMBLE
JOIN US!
GREEEE
WOOOOOOOOOO
GLARE
HAP-PENING ONCE EVERY 44 YEARS...
CHAPTER 1 MONSTER GAME

THE GAMES ARE ABOUT TO BEGIN.

CHAPTER 1
MONSTER GAME

CHEE CHITTER CHEE
CHEE CHITTER CHEE
FWUMP
HEY, IT'S SAN-SHIRO!
WHAT'S HE LUGGING AROUND?
HEY!
OFF ON ANOTHER BIG ADVEN-TURE ?!

YEAH! WANNA COME ALONG?
SNICKER
YOU'RE IN THE FIFTH GRADE AND YOU STILL GO ON ADVENTURES?! WHAT A BABY...
HA HA HA, HA HA HA
HA HA
HEY—!
GRR
YOU'RE NEVER TOO OLD FOR ADVEN-TURES!
LOOK AT ALL THE KID ADVENTURERS IN BOOKS AND MOVIES...!
IT'S NOT THAT!
IT'S IMPOSSIBLE ON THIS TINY ISLAND!

YOU NEVER KNOW! THERE COULD BE SOME AWESOME RUINS OR AN UNDIS-COVERED CREATURE HIDDEN SOME-WHERE!
OR MAYBE A GATEWAY TO ANOTHER WORLD!
SURE...
...IN YOUR DREAMS!
WELL, I'M GOING!
AND WHEN I MAKE A HUGE DIS-COVERY, YOU'LL SEE!
...
WHY IS HE SO CRAZY ABOUT ADVEN-TURES?
HIS DAD IS SOME FAMOUS EXPLORER.
MUST BE IN HIS BLOOD.
BUT HE'LL NEVER FIND ANY REAL ADVENTURES AROUND HERE.
YEAH.
WE KIDS CAN'T EVEN GET OFF THIS ISLAND BY OURSELVES.

CHITTER CHEE
HMPH!
THEY JUST DON'T GET IT!
CHITTER CHEE
I'VE EXPLORED EVERY INCH OF THIS ISLAND FOR THE PAST FIVE YEARS!
I KNOW THAT AN ADVENTURE MIGHT BE HIDING ANYWHERE!
AND I'VE GOT A GOOD FEELING ABOUT TODAY!
IT'S SUCH A GREAT DA-
SLIP

SMACK
WSSSHHHHHH
AHHHHH!
KLUNK
WHA-?
OWWW ...
WHERE AM I...?
...

FHOOOOO
?!
WHOA!
I NEVER KNEW THERE WAS A CAVE HERE...
I DIS-COV-ERED IT!
RSTL
IT'S DEEP...
WONDER HOW FAR IT GOES...
WHOOO

I'M FINALLY ON A REAL ADVENTURE!
SOMETHING GREAT IS GONNA HAPPEN! I KNOW IT!
BA BMP
BA BMP
AN UNDISCOVERED WORLD LIES JUST AHEAD!
BA BMP
BA BMP
BA BMP
GLIMMER
THE EXIT!
YAAAAAAH!
AT THE END OF THE LIGHT IS...
A WHOLE NEW WORLD!
RUSTLE
FWOOOM

RSTL
AGHHHHHH!
CRASH
UNHH...
...
WAP
THIS... IS...

...
RIGHT BEHIND MY HOUSE.
THAT "MYSTERIOUS CAVE" JUST TOOK ME BACK HOME...
SIGH
...
MAN! I SPENT ALL DAY EXPLORING...
...BUT WOUND UP RIGHT BACK WHERE I STARTED.
HEY! SAN-SHIRO!
I'VE GOT SOME CHORES FOR YOU!
QUIT GOOFING OFF!
OH. GRANDPA...

GRANDPA...
CAN'T WE GO SOMEWHERE THIS SUMMER?
WHAT?!
SOMEWHERE OTHER THAN THIS ISLAND.
THIS IS THE BUSY SEASON! WE DON'T HAVE ANY TIME FOR TRIPS!
BUT DON'T YOU THINK IT'S WEIRD THAT PEOPLE WHO RUN AN INN HAVE NEVER TRAVELED ANYWHERE?
HMPH! HMPH!
WAH! WAH!
THEN CAN I TAKE A TRIP ON MY OWN? PLEASE?
I SAID NO!
IF YOU'RE THINKING OF FOLLOWING IN YOUR FATHER'S FOOTSTEPS, I WON'T LET YOU GO!
NYAH

BUT I WANT GO ON ADVENTURES JUST LIKE DAD!
I WANT TO GET OFF THIS ISLAND AND SEE THE WORLD!
WHY LEAVE THE ISLAND? I'VE NEVER SET FOOT OFF THIS ISLAND AND LOOK AT ME NOW—A GRAND OLD MAN!
Hmph!
THAT'S WHAT I *DON'T* WANT TO BE!
YOU CAN SEE THE WORLD WHEN YOU'VE GROWN UP.
VWIP VWIP
NOOO!
I CAN'T WAIT THAT LONG!
WHY ?
'CAUSE I WANT TO HAVE AN ADVENTURE *NOW*!
HOW CHILD-ISH!
WE CAN'T LET YOU GO ON A TRIP BY YOURSELF—WE'D BE WORRIED SICK.
WHY? 'CAUSE ...
ULP...
'CAUSE ...
YARRR!
...
You guys just don't understand!!

WHAT DO YOU THINK, DEAR?
SHOULD WE LET HIM RIDE THE FERRY JUST ONCE?
NO.
SAN-SHIRO IS JUST LIKE HIS FATHER.
IF WE LET THAT ADVENTURE-CRAZY BOY OFF THE ISLAND...
IF THAT HAPPENS...
HE MIGHT NEVER COME BACK... LIKE HIS FATHER.
GLOOM
YES, IT'D BE SO LONELY HERE.
AH, NO! WHAT I MEANT IS...!
THERE WOULD BE NO ONE TO TAKE OVER THE INN!
...
SLURP

GEEZ...
THEY TREAT ME LIKE A BABY.
I JUST WANT TO GO ON ADVEN-TURES.
...LIKE YOU, DAD.
ADVEN-TURES ARE FUN, SAN-SHIRO!
I GOT YOU A SOUVENIR, SAN-SHIRO!
TA DAH!
WOW!
IT'S MAM-MOTH MEAT, SAN-SHIRO!
TA DAH!
AWE-SOME!
IT'S THE TOMB OF AN ANCIENT KING, SANSHIRO!
ARGH!
DA DO-O-OM
YOU'RE THE BEST, DAD!
JUST YOU WAIT, DAD!
I'M GONNA BE A GREAT ADVEN-TURER. JUST LIKE YOU!
AWW!
TAKE IT BACK!
TAKE IT BACK!

BUT FIRST, HOW DO I GET OFF THIS ISLAND?
STOW AWAY ON THE FERRY...?
BUILD A RAFT...?
WHAT AWESOME IDEAS!
SORRY, GRANDPA...
...BUT I'M NOT WASTING MY SUMMER HELPING AT THE INN.
Adventure! Adventure!
TUG
I WANT TO GO ON AN ADVENTURE *NOW*.
AN EPIC ADVENTURE THAT'S TOTALLY AWESOME!

DO YOU REALLY WANT AN ADVENTURE?
?
IF SO, JUST PEEL OFF A SEAL...
WHA-?!
WH-WHO'S THERE?
PEEL...
POOF
AGH!
PEEL OFF A SEAL...
FSH
FSH
FSH
FSH

WHOOOSH
WH-WHA-?
IF YOU WANT AN ADVENTURE, PEEL OFF A SEAL...
IF I PEEL THIS OFF...
...I'LL GET AN ADVENTURE?
QUIVER

ZMMM
WOBBLE
TUG
RIP
GULP
THAT IS YOUR STARTER KIT FOR THE GAME.
AND I...
...
?
!
PLOP
THUD
SLOO

ZAMM
AGYAAAWAH!!
SHHKKKKK

WH-WHO ARE YOU? HOW'D YOU GET IN HERE?
SWOOP
I AM FUE.
NO NEED TO CALL ME "MISTER" OR "SIR." JUST "FUE."
I AM YOUR GUIDE TO BAKÉ-GYAMON.
AND YOU?
YOUR NAME?
BAK... WHAT?
HUH ?!
SAN-SHIRO TAMON ...
YOU WISHED TO GO ON AN ADVENTURE...
THAT IS WHY I'M INVITING YOU TO JOIN THE GAME.
LOOM
J-JUST A MINUTE !
WHAT GAME ARE YOU TALKING ABOUT ?!

...
A GAME ORGANIZED BY MONSTERS FOR HUMANS...
A GAME CALLED... BAKÉ-GYAMON!
RUMBLE
A MONSTER GAME?!
COME ...
GRAB
I'LL TAKE YOU TO THE PLAYING FIELD.
VMMM
!

?!
WHAT THE-?! WE'RE FLYING!
SWOOSH
BY THE WAY, FUE... HOW DO YOU PLAY BAKÉ-GYAMON?
YOU'LL FIND OUT SOON ENOUGH...
SWOOSH
MY SCHOOL... IT LOOKS SO TINY!
WOW! I CAN SEE THE ENTIRE ISLAND!
...
THIS IS SO GREAT!
WOOHOO

SO, SAN-SHIRO ...
WHAT IS YOUR WISH?
MY WISH?
WHOEVER WINS AT BAKÉ-GYAMON...
...WILL BE GRANTED A SINGLE WISH.
MOST OF THE PARTICI-PANTS ARE AFTER THAT PRIZE...
...THOUGH THE WISHES VARY.
AND YOU? WHAT IS YOUR WISH?
...
I WANT ...

...NOTHING.
REALLY!
AS LONG AS I GET AN ADVENTURE, THAT'S ALL THAT MATTERS.
BY PLAYING THE GAME I'LL GET TO GO ON AN ADVENTURE, RIGHT?
...
ARE YOU **SURE**?
POWER, INFLUENCE, WEALTH... ANY OF THOSE COULD BE YOURS.
I KNOW THAT SOME ADVENTURERS SEEK TREASURES.
BUT THAT'S NOT ME.
DAD USED TO SAY...
AN ADVENTURE ISN'T ABOUT BECOMING RICH OR FAMOUS.

IT'S ABOUT OVER-COMING OBSTACLES AND REACHING YOUR GOAL.
THAT'S WHAT MAKES IT SO MUCH FUN.
THAT'S WHY *HAVING* THE ACTUAL ADVEN-TURE IS MY WISH.
NOTH-ING ELSE!
...
SO WHEN WILL WE GET TO THE PLAYING FIELD?
WE'RE ALREADY THERE.
HE'S NAÏVE. TOO NAÏVE...
HUH ?!
WHERE ? WHERE ?
NOT DOWN THERE. LOOK ABOVE YOU.

WHOO

WH-WHAT IS THAT?!
IT'S A BACKWARDS VERSION OF JAPAN.
RUMBLE
BACKWARDS JAPAN...
RUMBLE
RUMBLE
RUMBLE
THIS IS THE GAME FIELD FOR BAKÉGYAMON!
RUMBLE
LET'S GO...
THE OTHERS ARE WAITING.
FWHOO
WHOA!
SHKK

AH!
TUP
INHAAALE
PHEW
MY NEW ADVENTURE IS ABOUT TO BEGIN!
I FINALLY MADE IT OFF THE ISLAND!

YESS!
Adventure! Epic Adventure!
AWESOME! IT LOOKS JUST LIKE JAPAN!
WAP
YEAH!
THE BUILDINGS, TREES AND MOUNTAINS ARE IDENTICAL TO THOSE IN JAPAN.
URGG
YYY....
BUT THERE ARE NO PEOPLE HERE.
NO PEOPLE?
THAT WAY, THERE ARE NO DISTRACTIONS IN THE GAME.
ONLY CHILDREN...
...WHO WERE BROUGHT HERE BY GUIDES, LIKE MYSELF.

THE PLAYERS OF THE GAME.
THERE SURE ARE A LOT OF PLAYERS.
THIS IS GONNA BE SO MUCH FUN!
FUN, EH...
YOU'RE TAKING THIS LIGHTLY.
?
WHATEVER. I'M GONNA GO MEET THE OTHERS!
HEY!
MY NAME IS SAN-SHIRO TAMON!
NICE TO MEET YOU ALL!

...
SWIP
...
SWIP
SWIP
ARE YOU IGNORING ME?!
OF COURSE. LOOK AT THEM.
THEY'RE ALL HERE TO GET THEIR WISH GRANTED. THEY'RE PLAYING TO WIN!
YOU'RE THE ONLY ONE HERE THAT THINKS OF THIS AS "FUN."
YOU CAN'T WIN WITH THAT ATTI-TUDE.
I PICKED YOU BECAUSE I THOUGHT YOU SHOWED PROM-ISE.
APPARENTLY, I WAS MISTAKEN.

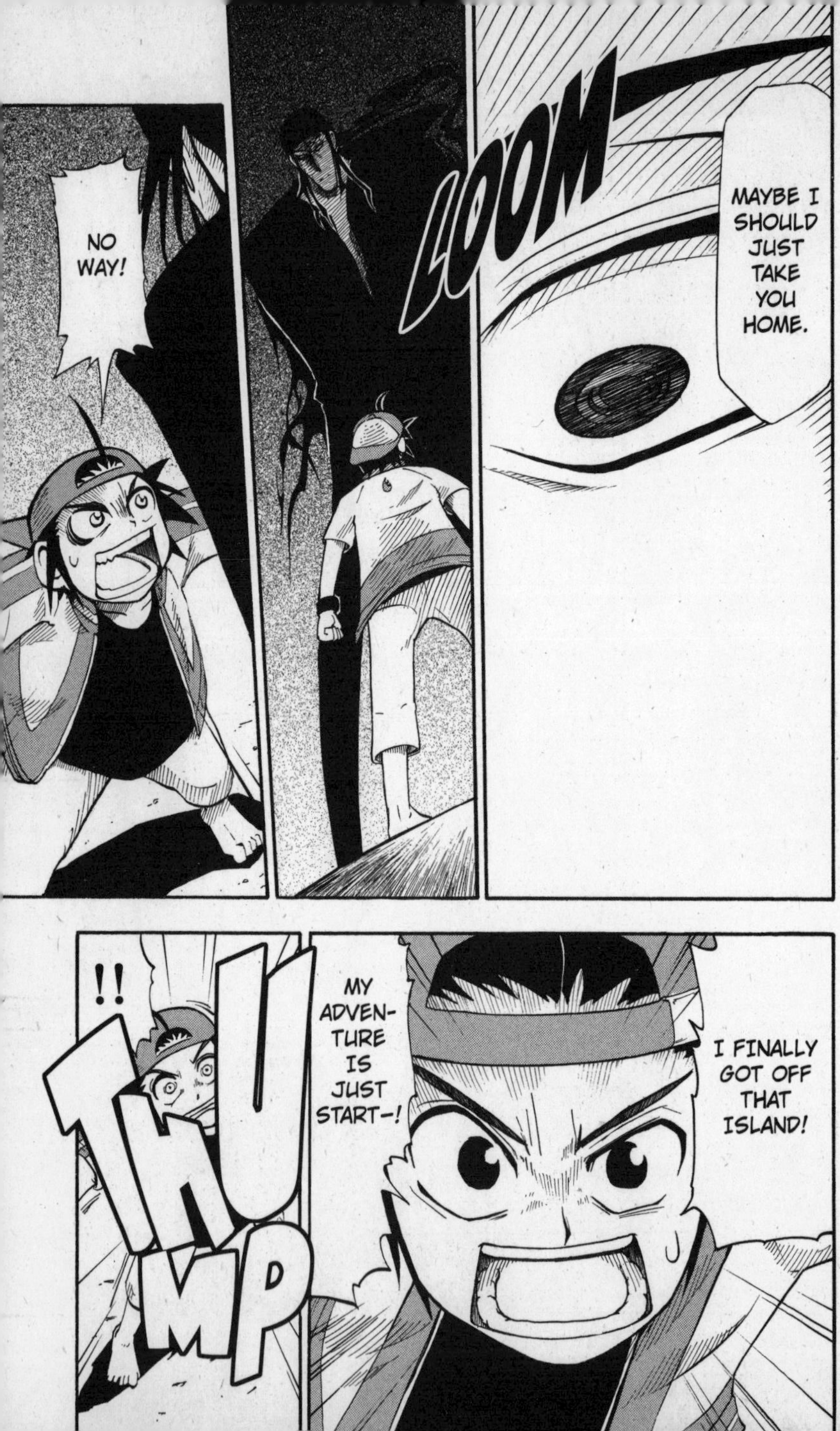
MAYBE I SHOULD JUST TAKE YOU HOME.
LOOM
NO WAY!
I FINALLY GOT OFF THAT ISLAND!
MY ADVENTURE IS JUST START-!
!!
THUMP

THUMP
THUMP
?!
IT'S HERE. GUESS WE'RE ABOUT TO BEGIN.
SAN-SHIRO ...

YOU'RE A FOOL!
YOU'RE A BRAT WITH A HEAD FULL OF SILLY DREAMS.
PEOPLE LIKE YOU MAKE ME SICK.
YOU CAN'T SURVIVE IN BAKÉ-GYAMON BY JUST WANTING TO HAVE FUN.
GIVE IT UP.
WELL *EXCUSE ME* FOR NOT KNOWING EVERY-THING!
THAT'S WHY I WANT TO GO ON ADVEN-TURES!

'CAUSE I'M NEVER GOING TO LEARN ON THAT ISLAND...
THAT'S WHY I WANTED TO GET OUT OF THERE.
I WANT TO MEET NEW PEOPLE!
I WANT TO SEE NEW THINGS!
I WANT TO SEE THE WORLD FOR MYSELF!
ISN'T THAT ENOUGH?!

NO ...
... IT'S NOT.
YOU'RE ONLY LOOKING AT THE SUPERFICIAL SIDE OF ADVENTURES.
THE REALITY OF IT IS TOUGHER ...
I KNOW.
?
I KNOW ADVEN-TURES AREN'T JUST FUN AND GAMES.
I *SAW* THAT...

...EVERY TIME I SAW MY DAD'S BACK!
I KNOW WHAT KIND OF HARD-SHIPS DAD FACED.
I KNOW HOW DANGEROUS THINGS CAN BE.

AND I STILL WANT TO GO ON ADVENTURES!
STOMP
I CAN'T HELP IT!
ISN'T THAT ENOUGH?
ISN'T IT ?!

...
WE WILL NOW BEGIN THE PRELIMINARY ROUND.
BZZZ
ZZZZT
ONLY THOSE WHO QUALIFY IN THIS ROUND CAN ADVANCE TO PLAY BAKÉ-GYAMON.
WH-WHAT WAS THAT?! THE SKY IS TALKING!
THE GAME IS ABOUT TO BEGIN!
MURMUR
...

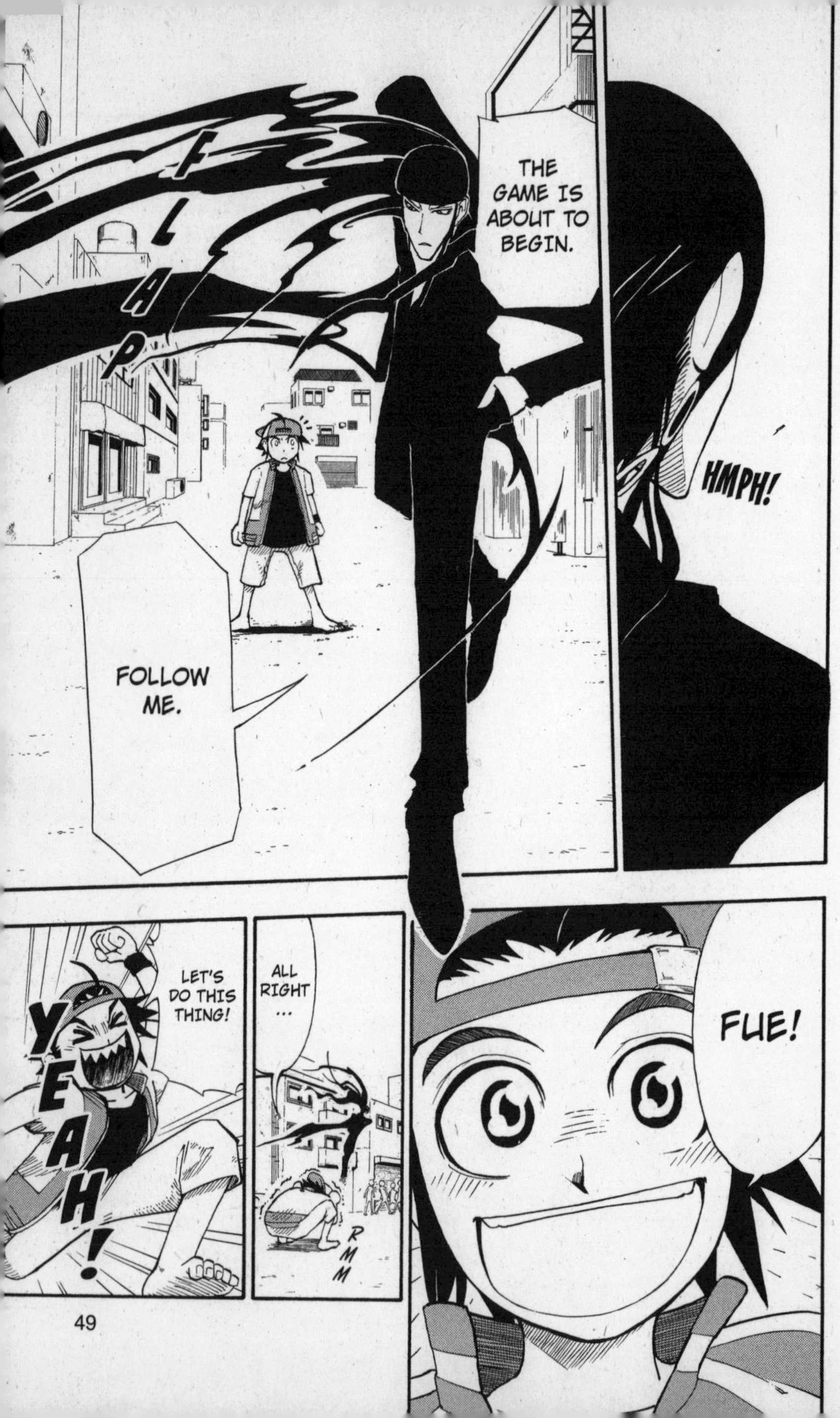
THE GAME IS ABOUT TO BEGIN.
HMPH!
FLAP
FOLLOW ME.
FUE!
ALL RIGHT ...
RMM
LET'S DO THIS THING!
YEAH!

FOR THE PRELIMINARY ROUND OF BAKÉ-GYAMON...
"OGRE TAG" WILL NOW BEGIN!

CHAPTER 2
GEKI BAN AND GEKI FU

WE'RE PLAYING TAG WITH A *REAL* OGRE?!
TO QUALIFY, YOU MUST ...
... TOUCH THE OGRE'S HORN.
DMM
ONLY THOSE WHO TOUCH ITS HORN...
...CAN MOVE ON TO THE NEXT GAME.
SO...
IF NO ONE SUCCEEDS, THEN ALL ARE DISQUALIFIED.

THAT'S SO CRAZY! JUST WHAT I'D EXPECT FROM MONSTERS!
MURMUR
PLAYING TAG WITH A REAL OGRE?
HOW CAN WE BEAT SOMETHING THAT HUGE?!
MURMUR
DASH
C'MON, GUYS! LET'S GO!!
IS HE SERIOUS?!
HE'S GOING IN COM-PLETELY UNARMED!
RAH!!
TUT TUT TUT
WAIT!
?!
WHERE IS YOUR SEAL AND STARTER KIT?
TH-THOSE THINGS THAT SHOWED UP IN MY ROOM?
RUSTLE
YOU MEAN, THIS...
FLAP
...AND THIS?
SWP

THE SEAL IS CALLED A "GEKI FU."
IT IS A CARD USED BY PLAYERS TO SUMMON A MONSTER ALLY.
A MONSTER ALLY?!
HOW DO I GET IT OUT?!
TELL ME!
JUST USE IT TOGETHER WITH YOUR STARTER KIT, THE "GEKI BAN."
LOOK!
?!
APPEAR!
SWIPE
FLASH
SWIRL
RUMBLE

HOWWWWL
GRRR
M-ME, TOO!
SWIPE
APPEAR!
COME ON OUT!
A MONSTER REALLY CAME OUT OF THE CARD!
!!
HMPH!
FLASH
SWIPE
VWOOSH

TUP
DMM
RMMM
LOOK AT ALL THE DIFFERENT MONSTERS!
WOW!
MAYBE NOW WE CAN TAKE ON THAT HUGE OGRE!
WHAT KIND OF COOL MONSTER WILL COME OUT OF MY GEKI FU?
YOU'LL SEE ...

IT DEPENDS ON YOUR CARD. THE POSSI- BILITIES ARE INFINITE.
THE QUALITIES *YOUR* MONSTER WILL HAVE...
... DEPENDS ON YOUR LUCK.
LUCK, HUH...?
SWIP
ALL RIGHT!
COME OUT, MONSTER !!
SWSHH
FWOOOM!!
...
BA-BMP BA BMP

TA-DAH
IT'S SO PUNY.
SHOCK!

IT TAKES THREE OF THEM TO EQUAL JUST ONE OF THE OTHER MONSTERS.
THEY'RE WEAK AND NOT SUITED FOR BATTLES.
OH ...
S-SORRY!
WHIMPER
THEY ARE CALLED "DORO-KOZO."
SORRY, SORRY.
SOME-TIMES I SPEAK WITHOUT THINKING!
"DORO" MEANS "MUD" AND "KOZO" MEANS "BOY."
GRR
SCREECH
RRMMM
YEAH, THEY DON'T SEEM AS TOUGH AS THE OTHER MONSTERS.
GROWL
I DIDN'T SAY THAT I DON'T WANT YOU!
HA HA HA HA
OH, COME ON!
BOING
BOING
WILT
GUESS YOU DREW A DUD.
SHOCK

WE GOT PAIRED UP BY CHANCE, BUT I'M HERE FOR AN ADVENTURE. HOW ABOUT YOU?
WE'LL MAKE A GREAT TEAM IN THE GAME, DORO-KOZO!
TOGETHER WE'LL BEAT THAT OGRE!
YEAH
STOMP
STOMP
STOMP
...
HUH?
SKIF SKIF
HEY...
SHUF SHUF

ZZM MMM
STOMP!
IT'S TOO BIG! THERE'S NO WAY WE CAN EVEN REACH ITS HEAD.
BUT WE HAVE TO TOUCH THE HORN TO BEAT IT...
92
WHAT-EVER! JUST ATTACK!
SLA
SH FWOOM

?
SCRATCH SCRATCH
?!
WHAT THE...? IT HARDLY NOTICED.
LET'S ALL ATTACK TO-GETHER !!
WSH
FWOOOM
VSH
ZTZTZT
RAT TAT TAT TAT TAT

GA HA HA HA!!
WHAM
WHAM
RATTATT
HA HA!
HE'S LAUGHING! WE'RE ONLY TICKLING HIM!
YOU CAN'T FIGHT HIM HEAD ON! USE YOUR BRAIN!
FIRST, CONFUSE HIM WITH DAZZLING SPEED!
FWASH
?!
ZP
ZP
ZZIP
ZIP
ZIP
YOU DON'T HAVE TO KNOCK HIM OUT... YOU CAN TRIP HIM TOO!
SHRRRRL

SRRKKKK
GRIP
WHOA!
ALL RIGHT!
EVERY-BODY HELP PULL!
YANK
TOUCH ITS HORN WHEN IT FALLS!
?
ONE, TWO, THREE... PULLLL!
IT'S STARTING TO TIP!
SWAY
KEEP PULLING!
?
TUG
PULL PULL
?
WHOA!

YANK!
!!
AGHHHH!
THUD
CRASH
GA HA HA HA
ROLL
SMACK
IT'S NO USE! WE CAN'T EVEN TRIP IT!
HOW'RE WE SUPPOSED TO BEAT SOMETHING THAT TOUGH?
...
THEN...

I GUESS IT'S UP TO US, DORO-KOZO!
DOOM
WHAT?!
ARE YOU OUT OF YOUR MIND?!
ALL OF THESE MONSTERS TOGETHER COULDN'T DO ANYTHING!
HOW CAN THOSE WEAK LITTLE THINGS DO IT?!
YOU NEVER KNOW UNTIL YOU TRY!
SHOCK SHOCK
RIGHT, DORO-KOZO?
WHIMPER
...

SEE? THEY KNOW THEY DON'T STAND A CHANCE.
YOU SCARED?
CONSIDERING THAT THE WINNER GETS THEIR WISH GRANTED, IT'S NOT GOING TO BE EASY TO WIN THIS GAME.
GIVE IT UP. YOU GOT UNLUCKY DRAWING THAT GEKI FU.
IT'D BE ANOTHER STORY IF THEY HAD SOME SPECIAL POWER.
POWERS, HMM...
REGULAR ATTACKS AREN'T GOING TO WORK ON THAT HUGE OGRE...
HMM...
HEY, KID! HEADS UP!
SHF
!!

CRASH
WH- WHAT'S GOING ON?!
WHOA!
BAM
ONE! TWO!
CRASH
THUD
SMASH
THREE! FOUR!
CRASH

CRUMBLE
DON'T JUST STAND THERE!
WATCH OUT!
SMASH
!
CRASH
WHAM
BAM
LET'S GET OUT OF HERE, GUYS!
HUH?
ARE WE MISSING ONE?
NUMBER THREE! WHERE ARE YOU?
SHOCK?!
WHIMPER

SQUASH
IT'S TRAPPED UNDER THAT RUBBLE!
HEY!
!
DASH
HOLD ON! I'LL SAVE YOU!
KRK

UNH!
...
WHAT'S HE DOING ...?
HE'LL NEVER WIN THE GAME LIKE *THAT*.
UNH ...
YOU'RE GOING TO GET SQUASHED IF YOU STAY THERE!
MY BUDDY IS TRAPPED UNDER HERE!
HELP ME OUT!
YOUR BUDDY? WHAT?
JUST GIVE IT UP! EVEN IF YOU DO MANAGE TO RESCUE IT...
...IT CAN'T HELP YOU WIN!
I'M NOT TALKING ABOUT THE GAME...

I NEED TO HELP MY FRIEND!
...
HEY! THE OGRE'S COMING!
!
STOMP
STOMP
STOMP
IF YOU DON'T GET OUT OF THERE, IT'LL SQUASH YOU!
DO YOU HEAR ME?
STOMP
STOMP
WHAT-EVER! WE ARE SO OUTTA HERE!

...
STOMP
STOMP
JUST A LITTLE MORE!
RRG
STOMP
LOOM
WATCH OUT!

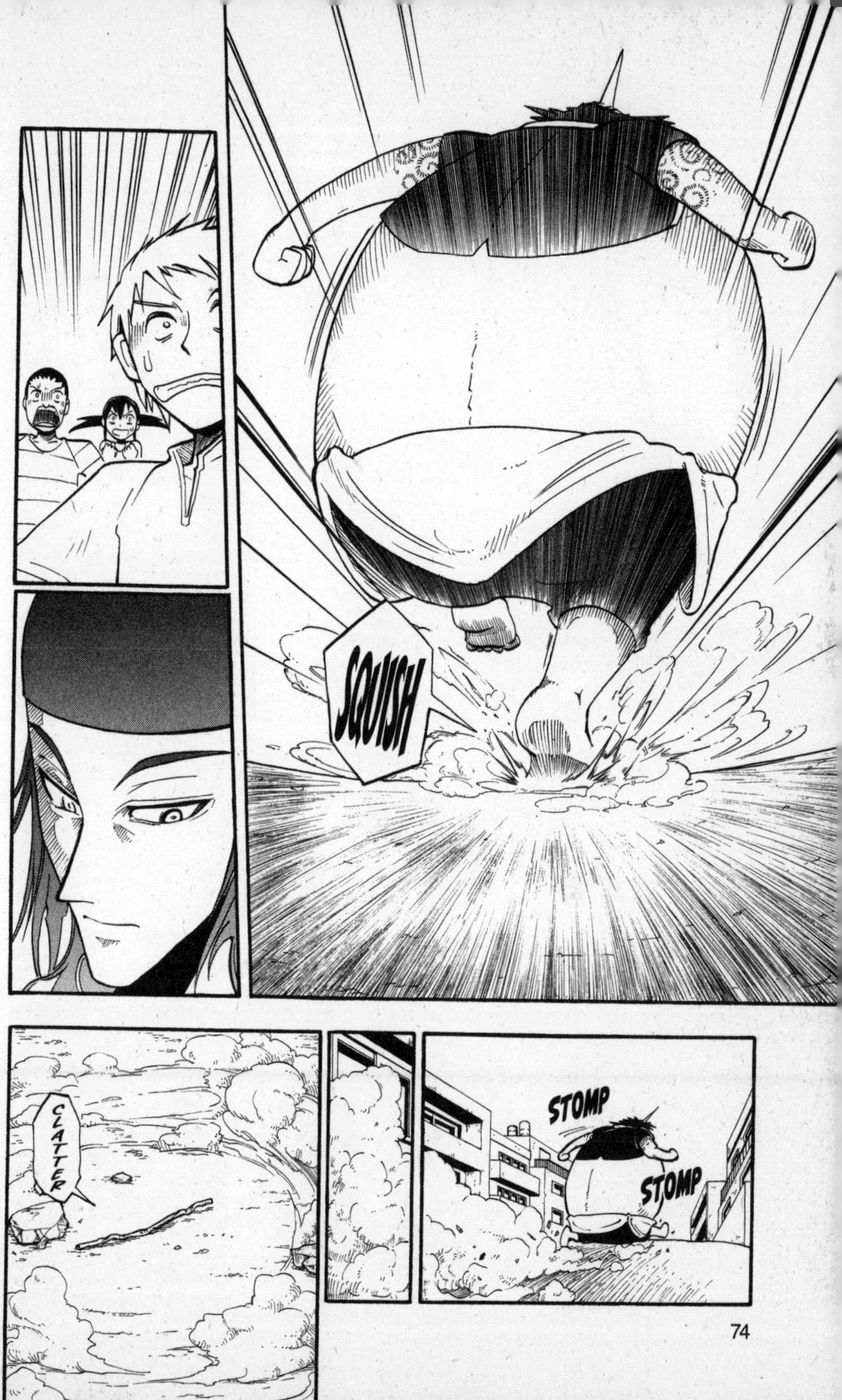
SQUISH
CLATTER
STOMP
STOMP

FLAP
TUP
WHAT A NAÏVE BOY...
WH... WHY?
COUGH
COUGH
AFTER DRAWING SUCH A WEAK MONSTER ...
...YOU SHOULD'VE STAYED ON THE SIDELINES SINCE YOU WERE GONNA LOSE ANYWAY.
WHAT -?!

YOU DON'T KNOW WHAT'LL HAPPEN UNTIL YOU TRY!
ONE.
TWO.
THREE.
ALL RIGHT. YOU'RE ALL HERE!
HEY! YOU'RE ALIVE!
WE THOUGHT YOU WERE A GONER!

NOW THAT THE THREE OF YOU ARE ALL BACK TOGETHER...
LET'S START OUR ATTACK AGAINST THAT OGRE!
DO YOU REALLY PLAN TO WIN THE GAME WITH THOSE THINGS?
OF COURSE!
BUT THEY NEARLY GOT YOU KILLED JUST NOW!
LOOK AT THEM! ANYONE CAN SEE THEY'RE WEAK AND WORTH-LESS!
HEY...!
STOP SAYING THAT!
NOW THEY'RE ALL SAD AGAIN!
WILT
HEY, DUMMY!
DON'T LISTEN TO HIM!
LIKE I TOLD YOU!

WE'RE GONNA PLAY THE GAME TOGETHER!
WE CAN WIN WITH TEAM-WORK!
GLEAM
OH, WAIT!
BUT YOU'RE AFRAID OF THE OGRE. WHAT'LL WE DO?
...

TUG
TUG
?
TUG
TUG
HMPH!
HAH!
YOU GUYS ...

ALL RIGHT! LET'S GO!
JUST YOU WAIT !!
WE'RE GOING TO GET OUR HANDS ON THAT HORN!

CHAPTER 3
AWESOME POWER

HEY, OGRE!
GLARE
POINT
YOUR HORN IS OURS!

YOU'RE GOING IT ALONE?! NOTHING WORKED EVEN WHEN ALL OF US ATTACKED TOGETHER!
WAH WAH
MAYBE HIS MONSTERS HAVE SOME AWESOME POWER!
HE'S OUR ONLY HOPE!
YOU CAN DO IT!
GO, DORO-KOZO!
SHOW THEM WHAT YOU CAN DO!
VWOOOOOM

WHAP
BONK
BONK
SLAP
SLAP
AAAAAAGH!
GRAAA
BAM
BAM
BAM
GOOD GRIEF!

OKAY! GUESS WE CAN'T FIGHT HIM HEAD ON...
PANT PANT
NO DUH!
IF YOU THREE DIDN'T STAND A CHANCE ...
MAYBE WE COULD TO DO IT IF THERE WERE MORE OF YOU...
NO WAY!
WA DI DA
HEY, WHERE'RE YOU GOING?
HFF HFF
ROLL ROLL
WHAT'S WITH ALL THOSE MUD BALLS?
PAT PAT

POP
POP
POP
POKE
WHOA!
THEY'RE MOVING!
PEEP!
POP
WMM WMM
THAT'S AN AWESOME POWER!!
HEH HEH!
NOW THERE'S EVEN MORE DORO-KOZOS!
WAH WAH

WITH THIS MANY, MAYBE WE CAN BEAT THAT OGRE!
NO, YOU CAN'T!
CLONES OF WEAK MONSTERS ARE STILL WEAK!
OH YEAH. YOU GUYS AREN'T REALLY MADE FOR COMBAT.
THOSE WITH STRONG MONSTERS FOUGHT TOGETHER AND STILL FAILED.
THOSE PUNY THINGS DON'T HAVE A CHANCE!
YOU CAN'T DO IT. THERE'S NO WAY YOU'LL BE ABLE TO TOUCH THE HORN...
...
TOUCH THE HORN...
!
I'VE GOT IT!!

WE DON'T NEED TO BEAT OR TRIP THAT THING.
I JUST HAVE TO TOUCH HIS HORN!
I'M A GENIUS!
CAN'T BE DONE!
THE BUILDINGS AROUND HERE AREN'T AS TALL AS THAT OGRE.
WRONG!
THERE'S NO WAY YOU CAN REACH IT.
IT'S HOPELESS UNLESS WE BEAT IT DOWN.
OH, THERE'S A WAY...
... WITH THE HELP OF THESE GUYS!
BAM
?
?
?

STOMP
STOMP
STOMP
LOOKS LIKE THEY'VE ALL GIVEN UP.
SO NO ONE QUALIFIES...
HEY! OVER HERE, YOU BIG OGRE!

I'VE GOT A MONSTER THAT'S EVEN TALLER THAN YOU!
WHOOOM!

HAHAHA!
YOU SCARED NOW?!
I'M NOT DONE YET...
...
JUST 'CAUSE YOUR MONSTER'S TALLER DOESN'T MEAN ANYTHING...
BUT WE HAVE TO TOUCH THE HORN OURSELVES!
DASH
WOBBLE
?!
STRETCH
I'M GOING AFTER THAT HORN!!
STRETCH

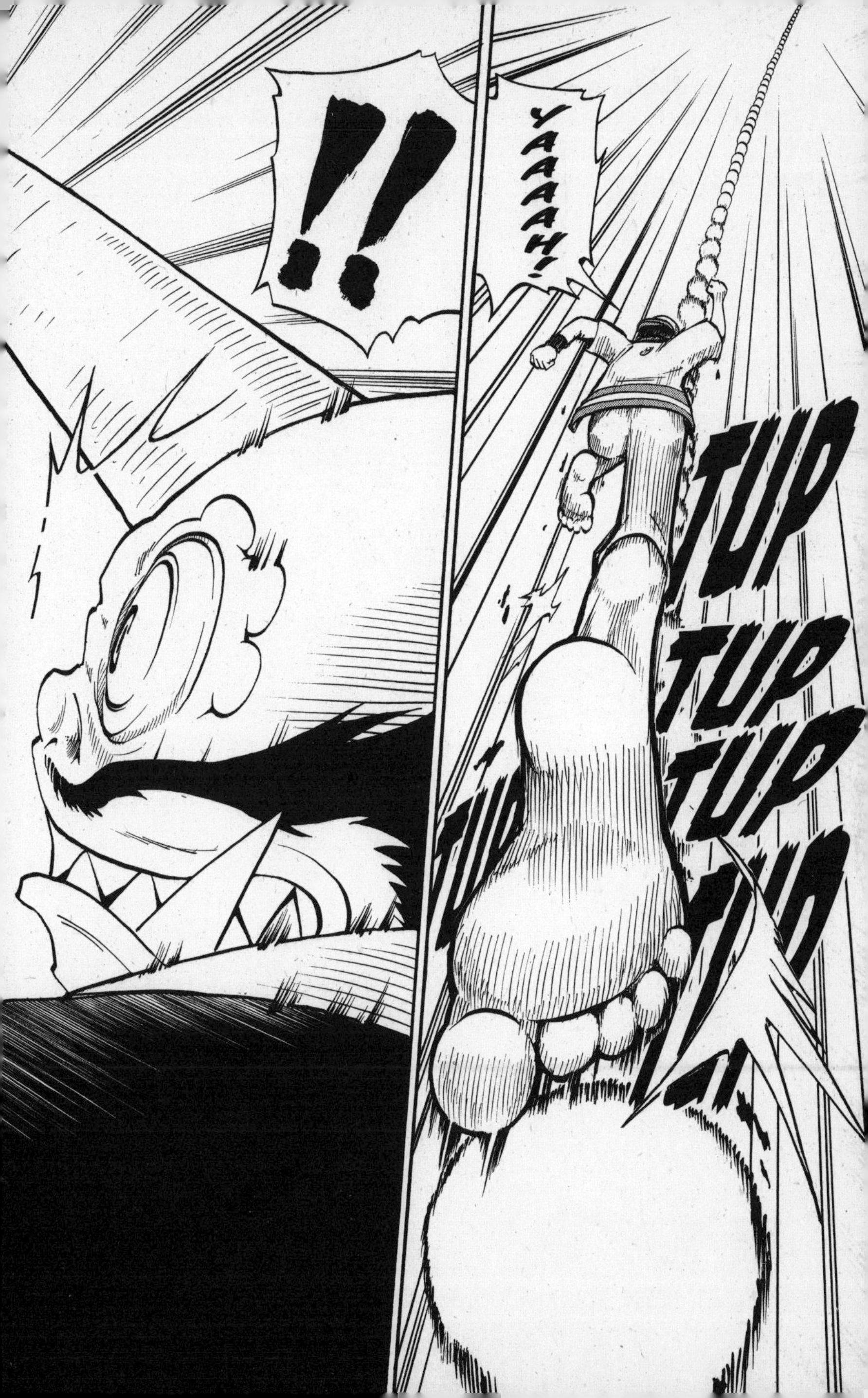
!!
YAAAAAH!
TUP TUP TUP TUP

YOUR HORN IS MINE!
LEAP

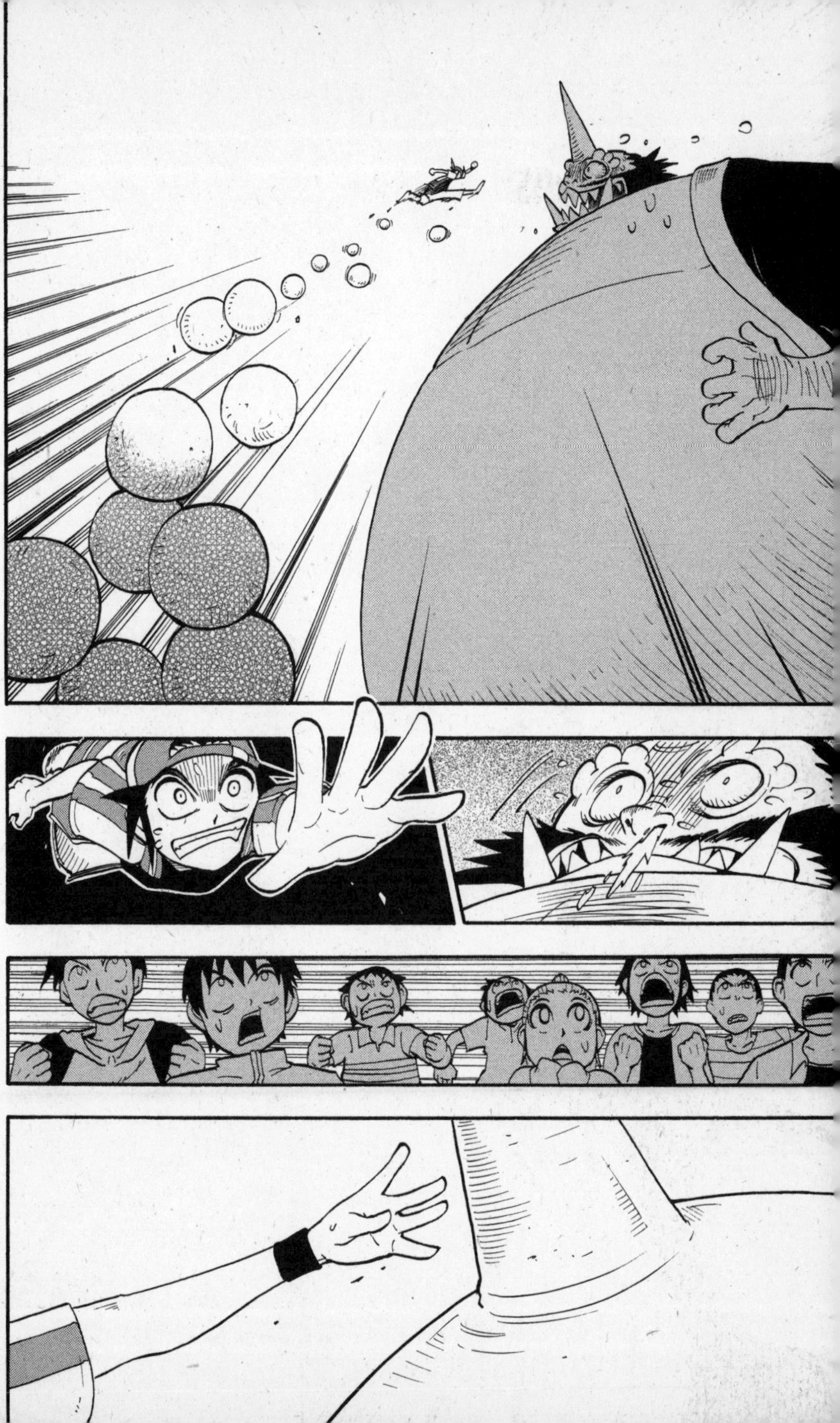

SWISH
WIP
?!
NOOOOOOOOO...
?!
GRAB
I'M NOT DONE YET!
UHN!

!!!
YANK
YANK
!!
!
TOMP TOMP
SHAKE
SHAKE
AHHHHH!
WHIMPER
STOMP
STOMP
ZOOM
BAM
SPLAT

SLIP
DORO-KOZO!
WOBBLE
AGHHH!
CRASH

... DORO-KOZO ...
THUD!
SNAP
BLUB BLUB
YOU'RE ALL SQUASHED... I'M SO SORRY...
POK POK
POP
RAH RAH
...
THAT'S GREAT!
DOROKOZO! YOU'RE ALL RIGHT!

...
MURMUR MURMUR
C'MON! GET OVER HERE!
HUH? WHAT?
YOU'RE THE ONE THAT DID IT...
...SO YOU SHOULD TOUCH IT FIRST.
EVERY-ONE'S WAITING FOR YOU.
OH RIGHT, THE HORN!
GO ON ...

SLAP
HURRAH!
YAAAAYYY!

WOO HOO!
NOW IT'S OUR TURN!!
WHOA!
SLAP
SLAP
SLAP
GRIN
RAHHHHHH
WE ALL PASSED THE PRELIMINARY ROUND!
YAYYY
WE DID IT, DORO-KOZO!
ALL THANKS TO YOU GUYS!

EVERY-ONE PASSED THE QUALI-FIER...
WELL, IT IS ONLY THE PRELIMI-NARIES.
YAAAYYY
SANSHIRO TAMON... WHAT A STRANGE KID.

BAKÉGYAMON EXTRA COMIC

THE END

CHAPTER 4
THE ONE TO BEAT

OKAY, I GUESS I'LL TAKE THESE.
SQUEAK
SQK
SQK
Y'KNOW...
MUNCH
CRUNCH
AHHH
PLUCK
CRACKERS
IT'S WEIRD BEING IN A DESERTED TOWN.
TMP TMP
WHOOO

IT WAS FUN AT FIRST JUST RUNNING AROUND!
BUT NOW IT'S GETTING KINDA LONELY!
YAHOO!
RAAAAH!!
I FINALLY MADE SOME FRIENDS...
BUT THERE WAS A WEIRD BLINDING LIGHT AND WE ALL GOT SEPARATED.
AND THE DORO-KOZO TURNED BACK INTO A GEKI FU TOO.
THIS'D BE A LOT MORE FUN IF THEY WERE STILL AROUND.
HEH HEH!
ROLL

MAN...
I HOPE THE NEXT GAME STARTS SOON.
WHAK WHAK
YOU WILL NOW TRAVEL ACROSS BACKWARDS JAPAN...
...CHALLENGING RIVAL PLAYERS TO GAMES OF BAKÉGYAMON.
THOSE WHO LOSE ARE ELIMINATED... AND THE GAME CONTINUES UNTIL THERE IS ONLY ONE LEFT.
I'LL ALWAYS BE NEAR...
...CHECKING ON YOUR PROGRESS TO SEE IF YOUR "ADVENTUROUS HEART"...
...CAN GET THE JOB DONE!
RIVALS... HUH.
TWANG
HM?
TWANG
WHAT WAS THAT?

OH!
TWAING
TWANG
TWAING
BAM
HEY!
TUT
TUT

ARE YOU A PLAYER? WHAT'S YOUR NAME?
...
TOSHIO SAEGUSA.
HI, I'M SANSHIRO TAMON!
LET'S BE FRIENDS!
NO.
AS IF!
HUH?
I DIDN'T COME HERE TO MAKE FRIENDS.
BESIDES ...

YOU CAN'T HOPE TO UNDERSTAND A ROCKER LIKE ME.
...I WALK ALONE.
GLINT
...
WHA ...?
OHHH... YOU LIKE THE PUNK-ROCK LOOK!
I GET IT!
PING
IT'S NOT A "LOOK"! I *AM* A ROCKER!
HMM... A ROCKER, HUH...
WH-WHAT?
OKAY, I'VE GOT IT!

YOU'RE "LONDON"!
I'M GONNA CALL YOU LONDON!
PFFT
YOU CAN'T JUST GIVE ME A NICK-NAME!
WELL, YOU'VE GOT A UNION JACK BANDANA.
THAT'S NOT WHAT I MEANT ...!
YOU MUST LIKE LONDON! ♥
I'M GONNA CALL YOU LONDON FROM NOW ON!
YOU JUST TOTALLY BLEW MY COOL...
NICE TO MEET YOU, LONDON! LET'S BE FRIENDS!
GLOOM
HMPH! WHATEVER!
I'LL PROBABLY NEVER SEE YOU AGAIN ANYWAY...
LATER!

WHAT ARE YOU TALKING ABOUT?
I GAVE YOU A NICKNAME, SO WE'RE BEST FRIENDS NOW!
RIGHT
YOU'RE NOT THE BOSS OF ME!
GRR
CALM DOWN... BE COOL... KEEP COOL...
I JUST HAVE TO IGNORE HIM!
NOW YOU HAVE TO GIVE ME A NICKNAME.
GRIN
YOU DESERVE THE LAMEST NICKNAME EVER...
...BUT I'M SO COOL THAT I CAN'T THINK OF ANY STUPID-SOUNDING NAMES!
GO ASK SOME-ONE ELSE.
TUT TUT
STOMP
GO AWAY!

OH, HEY ...
WHAT'S YOUR WISH, LONDON ?
FLINCH
I...
I WANT TO BECOME A BIG STAR AND ROCK OUT ALL OVER THE WORLD!
I JOINED BAKĒGYAMON TO MAKE THAT DREAM COME TRUE.
ONLY ONE PERSON CAN WIN AND HAVE HIS WISH GRANTED...
...SO I DON'T NEED ANY FRIENDS!
OH.

IF YOU'RE GONNA BE A ROCK STAR...
...PLAY ME A SONG.
YOU WANT TO HEAR?
YEAH!
INHALE
I'M A LONE WOLF JUST A-HOWLIN' LIKE A TYPHOON!
ZM ZM
TWAAANG
ZMM ZM
WELL?

Y-YOU'RE AWFUL.
S-SORRY.
GLOOM
NO, I KNOW THAT I'VE GOT A UNIQUE MUSICAL STYLE...
THAT'S WHY I'M HERE!
MY SOUL IS OVERFLOWING WITH ROCK 'N' ROLL, BUT I CAN'T EXPRESS IT WITH MY VOICE!
DO YOU KNOW WHAT A BIG LOSS THAT IS TO THE MUSIC WORLD?!
ROCKIN' SOUL
SPLASH
STARE

THAT'S WHY I'VE *GOT* TO WIN.
I'LL CRUSH ANYONE WHO GETS IN MY WAY, ESPECIALLY TWERPS LIKE YOU!
...
LOOKS LIKE WE'RE HERE.
SHEEEN
...THE SITE OF THE NEXT GAME.

WOOOOOOOH
OKAY, IT LOOKS LIKE YOU'RE ALL HERE.
SO...
LET'S START BAKĒ-GYAMON!
WHOA!
THE VOICE FROM THE SKY!
WAIT.
IT SOUNDS CLOSER THAN LAST TIME.

WELL I AM PRETTY CLOSE ...
SEE?
LOOM
AHHH!
HA HA HA
HA
HA HA HA
FLOAT
MY NAME IS NEID...
FLOAT

I AM THE HOST OF BAKÉ-GYAMON ...
I'M NEID. NICE TO MEET YOU ALL! ♡
BYOING
THE HOST?
YOU?
YES! ♥
THE GAME IS "SHADOW STEPPING" ...
YOU ALL KNOW IT, RIGHT?
YOU HAVE TO KEEP THE PERSON WHO'S "IT" FROM STEPPING ON YOUR SHADOW.
BUT IN BAKÉ-GYAMON, IT'S A LITTLE DIFFERENT...
FIRST, EVERYONE GATHER AT THE STARTING POINT.
FLOAT
THEN PICK A PARTNER.
A PARTNER?
THIS GAME IS PLAYED IN TWO-PERSON TEAMS.
FOR YOUR PARTNER ...
...YOU SHOULD CHOOSE ...
TWIST TWIST

...THE PERSON THAT YOU WANT TO BEAT MORE THAN ANYONE.
...
I PICK HIM!
WHAT ?!
YOU CAN'T! WE'RE BEST FRIENDS!
HAHAHAHAHA
CRACK
JERK!
NO! YOU JUST DECIDED THAT ON YOUR OWN!
I WANT YOU OUT OF HERE AS SOON AS POSSI-BLE!
LET ME EXPLAIN THE GAME.

KRAK
THE RULES ARE SIMPLE!
KRIK
RUMBLE RUMBLE
!!!
CROSS THE FIELD AND STEP THROUGH THE TORII GATE. DO THAT AND YOU PASS THIS ROUND!
BOOM
YOU HAVE ONE HOUR.
YOU ALL HAVE THE SAME GEKI FU...
AND THIS TIME, YOU CAN SUMMON IT AS MANY TIMES AS YOU WANT.
THE CARDS HAVE BEEN GIVEN OUT.
USE IT WISELY.

WHAT ?!
I SUGGEST THAT YOU COOPERATE WITH YOUR PARTNER.
GIGGLE
LONDON!
BE QUIET
TEAMWORK IS CRUCIAL FOR THIS PARTICU-LAR GAME.
OH YES, ONE LAST THING.
HEE HEE
PAT PAT
GLOOM
COOPERATE?!
... WITH *HIM*?!
C'MON, LONDON! WE'LL MAKE A GREAT TEAM!

THE GAME FOR THIS ROUND IS...
"SHADOW STEPPING!"
FLOAT
THE RULES ARE SIMPLE! ♡
JUST CROSS THE FIELD.
PASS THROUGH THAT TORII GATE AND YOU'VE CLEARED IT.
ZOOM
CHAPTER 5 TWO MAKE A TEAM
YOU CAN GO THROUGH THE GOAL ALONE...
...BUT YOU'RE GOING TO WORK IN PAIRS!
TWO
TWO
BETTER PLAY NICE WITH YOUR TEAM-MATE! ♡

PLAY NICE?
BUT THIS GUY IS SO UNCOOL!
HIC
C'MON, LONDON! WE'LL BEAT THIS IN NO TIME WITH THE POWER OF OUR FRIENDSHIP!
BRING IT ON!
CHAPTER 5 TWO MAKE A TEAM

REMEMBER, YOU ONLY HAVE ONE HOUR.
BETTER GET GOING!
POOF
!
I'M FIRST!
IT'LL ONLY TAKE FIVE MINUTES TO GET OVER THERE!
DASH
OH NO! WE NEED TO GET GOING TOO, LONDON!
TUT TUT
WAIT!
?!
SWIP
JUST WATCH!
TUT TUT
GURGLE

OOOOM
URGLE

HAARG
FW

CHOMP
WHOA !
IT ATE HIM!
MUNCH
PTOO
SPLAT
BLOOP
EWWW !
SEE? THAT'S WHAT HAPPENS WHEN YOU JUMP IN WITHOUT THINKING FIRST.
GIGGLE
MURMUR
MURMUR

SWSSSSH
IN THIS GAME, THERE ARE LOTS OF MONSTERS CALLED "SUIJIN" SWIMMING AROUND.
"SUI" MEANS "WATER" AND "JIN" MEANS "GOD".
THEY'LL SWALLOW ANYTHING THEY SEE MOVING.
GLARE
GLARE
THEN HOW'RE WE SUPPOSED TO GET TO THE GOAL?!
THERE'S A WAY.
THE SUIJIN DON'T REACT TO THINGS THAT ARE IN THEIR SHADOWS.
AS LONG AS YOU'RE IN THEIR SHADOWS, THE SUIJIN CAN'T MOVE.
FREEZE
SO...
...THAT...
...MEANS...

GOAL!
JUST STAY UNDER THE SUIJINS' SHADOWS AND HEAD TOWARDS THE GOAL.
THAT'S WHY IT'S CALLED "SHADOW STEPPING." GET IT?
GOT IT. BACK OFF, BUDDY...
I ALMOST RAN OUT THERE...
HOW DID YOU KNOW IT'D BE DANGEROUS, LONDON?
LOOM
THERE'S NO WAY THE GAME WOULD BE THAT EASY.
THERE HAD TO BE SOME KIND OF TRAP.
IF NOT, WE WOULDN'T NEED THESE GEKI FU!
FWIP
IN BAKĒGYAMON YOU NEED TO STAY COOL AND JUDGE EACH SITUATION AS IT ARISES.
COOL!!
HEY!
ARE YOU LISTEN-ING?!
HUH?

HEY! EVERYONE ELSE HAS STARTED!
WHAP
LET'S GET GOING!
I'M GOING BY MYSELF.
SMAK
YOU'RE ON YOUR OWN!
?
IF ALL WE HAVE TO DO IS MOVE BENEATH THEIR SHADOWS, I CAN DO THIS ALONE.
IT'S NOT LIKE WE BOTH HAVE TO GET TO THE GOAL.
A CLUELESS KID LIKE YOU WILL JUST GET IN MY WAY.
YOU'LL THROW OFF MY *COOL* JUDGMENT!
LONDON ...

SWSH
JUST WATCH!
WE JUST HAVE TO STEP ON THE SHADOWS, RIGHT?!
COME ON! I CAN DO THIS THING TOO!
HUH?
ALONE...
PANT
PANT
SWOOSH
TUT TUT
NOW!
DASH
YAAAAAA!
DH-DH DH DH DHDHDH

FLOAT
CHOMP
PLOP
THIS IS GONNA BE HARD.
I DIDN'T EXPECT THEM TO MOVE SO QUICKLY...
PANT
PANT
PHEW, THAT WAS CLOSE.
PANT
PANT
WAIT! WHERE'S LONDON ?!
THE OTHERS SEEM TO BE HAVING A HARD TIME TOO...
CHOMP
CHOMP
AHHHH

DASH
TUP
TUP
TUP
SHHF
WHOA!
YOU'RE AWESOME, LONDON!
HOW DO YOU DO IT?
IT'S EASY.
EACH SUIJIN MOVES IN A SPECIFIC PATTERN.
SEE HOW IT MOVES AND WHERE IT'S HEADED. IT'S A MATTER OF TIMING...
I GET IT. OBSERVATION, HUH...
OKAY! HERE I GO!
STARE

!
GLARE
THERE!
DASH
TURN
YIKES!
AHHH!
GRAAH
WHOMP
PUFF
PUFF
FSHH

BAM
WOW ... THAT WAS CLOSE.
SERIOUSLY... YOU ARE SO UNCOOL!
PANT
PANT
PLEASE! STOP MESSING UP MY TIMING!
IT'S JUST THAT THE SUIJIN DIDN'T MOVE LIKE I THOUGHT IT WOULD.
EACH SUIJIN MOVES IN A DIFFERENT PATTERN.
YOU HAVE TO WATCH EACH ONE CLOSELY.
WOW, THAT SOUNDS HARD...
BUT I'LL DO BETTER NEXT TIME!
YEAH!
...
HOW ...

HOW CAN YOU HAVE FUN AT A TIME LIKE THIS?
HM?
'CAUSE IT *IS* FUN!
GRIN
I MEAN, LOOK! THERE'S A FISH THAT CAN SWALLOW A PERSON WHOLE!
AND IT'S SWIMMING THROUGH THE AIR! ISN'T THAT AWESOME?!
WOOHOO!♥
HAVING AN ADVENTURE LIKE THIS...
HOW COULD I *NOT* HAVE FUN?
AREN'T YOU HAVING FUN, LONDON?
?!
YOU'RE ALWAYS SO GRUMPY.

IT'LL BE MORE FUN...
...IF YOU ENJOY IT!
NO, DUH!
OF COURSE IT'S MORE FUN IF YOU ENJOY SOME-THING!
ANYONE KNOWS THAT!
I JUST MEANT THAT YOU'LL ENJOY YOURSELF MORE.
HA HA HA
IF WE CAN CLEAR THIS GAME TOGETHER ...
...I'M SURE WE'D BOTH HAVE MORE FUN!
IT'D BE MORE FUN TOGETHER? WHAT IS HE TALKING ABOUT?
NOW WHICH SHADOW SHOULD I GO AFTER NEXT?
...

I TOLD HIM TO GET LOST, BUT HE STILL WANTS TO BE MY FRIEND...
THAT ONE? OR THAT ONE?
OKAY, I PICK THAT ONE!
VIP
HE'S WEIRD ...
LET'S GO, LONDON!
WAIT!
GRAB

?
I'LL FIGURE OUT THE TIMING...
YOU JUST FOLLOW MY LEAD!
LONDON!

TUP
TUP
LONDON IS AMAZING!
TUP
HE'S FIGURED OUT THE MOVEMENTS OF EACH SUIJIN!
TUP
WE'RE MOVING FAST NOW!
CHAPTER 6 SACRIFICE
I'LL FIGURE OUT THE TIMING...
YOU JUST FOLLOW MY LEAD!
THIS'LL BE A PIECE OF CAKE...
STOP
SMACK

OW! WHAT THE...? WHY'D YOU STOP?
THE SHADOWS ...
HM?
THERE ARE NO MORE SHADOWS...
CHAPTER 6 SACRIFICE

WHAT?
YOU'RE RIGHT! STARTING HERE, THERE ARE NO MORE SUIJINS.
EMPTY
WE'LL BE ATTACKED IF WE STEP OUT FROM UNDER THE SHADOWS!
WHAT ARE WE GOING TO DO?
LONDON...
...
HEE HEE...
YOU ONLY HAVE 15 MINUTES LEFT.
TICK TOCK TICK TOCK
HURRY, HURRY!
FLOAT
DARN...
THEN WE'LL JUST HAVE TO...
HAHAHAHA

HEY! DON'T ...!
DASH
IT'S TOO FAR ...!
RUN ALL THE WAY TO THE GATE!
DASH
GLARE
GLARE
GLARE
IT'S A LONG SHOT, BUT...
RSTL
DM DM DM DM
SWSH
SWSH

SWIP
I HOPE THIS WORKS!
THE GEKI FU!
BEFORE THE GAME, EVERYONE WAS GIVEN THE SAME GEKI FU...
BUT THERE'S BEEN NO NEED TO USE IT SO FAR.
THEN...
DM DM
NOW'S THE TIME TO USE IT!
DM DM DM
TURN
HERE GOES!
SWIPE
DM DM DM DM

WOOO
POOF
KER-SPLASH
FSSHHHHHHHH
ALL RIGHT!

DM DM DM DM DM DM
THIS IS AWE-SOME!
IT'S A WATER FORCE FIELD!
FSSHHHHH
I CAN'T!
?!
I...
GREAT! NOW KEEP RUNNING TOWARD THE GOAL!
IT'S ... TOO MUCH!
THE WATER PRESSURE IS TOO MUCH! I CAN BARELY STAND UP, LET ALONE RUN!
RRG
ZMM
ZSHH
I CAN'T MOVE!

AGH!
SLIP
SPLISH
SPLASH
UNGH!
PLOP
HURRY UP! GET MOVING!
THEY'RE COMING AT YOU!
GRAAAAH
!!
UGH!
DASH
FWIP
GEKI FU!!

"SEN" MEANS "SPRING" AND "KAKU" MEANS "SHELL."

THAT DOESN'T SOLVE OUR PROBLEM!
WE WON'T CLEAR THIS GAME THAT WAY!
?
?
THAT FREAKY NEID SAID...
...THAT WE'D NEED TEAMWORK FOR THIS GAME...
FLOAT
FLOAT
...BUT HE ALSO SAID THAT WE DIDN'T HAVE TO REACH THE GOAL TOGETHER.
BECAUSE USING THE SENKAKU MAKES ITS USER IMMO-BILE...
...THE GAME IS RIGGED SO ONLY ONE TEAM MEMBER CAN MAKE IT TO THE GOAL!
DM DM D
WHAT ?!

THE PLAYERS WILL BE ATTACKED BY THE SUIJIN AS THEY RUN TOWARDS THE GOAL.
BUT IF THEY USE THE GEKI FU TO STOP THEM, THEY WILL GET STUCK BECAUSE OF THE WATER PRESSURE.
SO ONLY ONE PERSON CAN RUN TO THE GOAL WHILE THE OTHER HOLDS BACK THE SUIJIN...
TUT TUT
RRG
THAT'S THE ONLY WAY TO BEAT THIS GAME!
SO THE ONE WHO USES THE GEKI FU...
IT'S ALL OVER ONCE HE CAN'T HANDLE THE WATER PRESSURE.
LONDON! IF YOU KNEW THAT, WHY DID YOU HELP ME?!
DM DM DM DM
DM DM DM
WHA ...?
JUST 'CAUSE!
DID YOU THINK I WAS GONNA SAY THAT I COULDN'T LET DOWN MY FRIEND OR SOMETHING?
DON'T WORRY ABOUT ME...

I DON'T NEED ANYONE'S HELP.
I'LL FIND MY OWN COOL WAY TO THE GOAL.
NOW HURRY UP!
GO WHILE I'M HOLDING BACK THE SUIJIN!
DM DM
RRG
DM DM DM
LONDON!
WHAT?
YOU WANT TO CON-TINUE YOUR ADVEN-TURE, RIGHT?!
I CAN'T THINK OF A COOL PLAN WITH A PEST LIKE YOU AROUND!
SO GET OUTTA HERE!
RRG
LONDON ...

I WAS TOTALLY COOL UP TILL NOW...
...BUT MY ARMS ARE STARTING TO GO NUMB!
RRG
UGH!
DMDM DM
I GOTTA THINK OF A NEW PLAN...
...AND QUICK!
WOBBLE
RRG
4000OOM
THE GEKI FU!
POOF
OH NO!

SPLASH
?!
WHY DIDN'T YOU GO?
GRIN
JUST 'CAUSE!
BE-SIDES...
COPYCAT!
I DON'T LIKE GAMES WHERE YOU HAVE TO SACRIFICE ONE PLAYER FOR THE OTHER TO WIN!
LET'S GET TO THE GOAL TOGETHER!
SHOOP
OH MY.
FLOAT
SPLASH

I HAVE A PLAN!
GET ON MY SHOULDERS, LONDON!
GRAAH
WHAT?
JUST DO IT!
AND NOW TO USE MY GEKI FU...
FWIP
THAT WON'T CHANGE ANYTHING!
IT WILL IF I...
WOOOOO
...DO THIS!

VWOOSH
?!
NOW, LONDON!
SHOOT THAT ANNOYING NEID!
HUH?
DMDMDMDM DM DMDMDMDMDM
!
GOTCHA!
NO! PLEASE DON'T!
FWAP

FSSHH
EEK!
SPLOOSH
WHOOSH
SMACK
SHHKK
THUD

WE DID IT! WE GOT TO THE TORII GATE!
LOOOM!
JUST LIKE I PLANNED !!
OKAY, LONDON! C'MON!
AND ...
GOOOAAALLL!
TA DAH!
YEAH! WE DID IT!!
EVERYTHING YOU DO IS SO CRAZY!
AW, SHUCKS!
BUT ...
...THAT WAS PRETTY FUN.
GIGGLE GIGGLE

TIME! ALL THE WINNERS WILL NOW MOVE ON TO THE NEXT GAME SITE!
GLIMMER
FSST
HEY, LON-DON ...
SEE YOU AROUND!
...
YOU BETTER NOT GET DIS-QUALIFIED.
'CUZ THE NEXT TIME WE MEET...
I'M GONNA GIVE YOU THE DUMBEST NICKNAME *EVER*.

NOW THAT EVERY-ONE'S HERE...
LET'S GET ON WITH THE GAME!
CHAPTER 7 STRONG ONE
YOU'LL PAY FOR THAT!
?!
OH, IT'S THE BOY IN THE RED HAT...
WHY ARE YOU SO MAD?!
I SAID I WAS SORRY!
IT'S GOING TO GET LIVELY AGAIN.
GIGGLE
SAYING SORRY DOESN'T CUT IT!
THIS IS WHY I HATE BOYS!

I DON'T CARE WHAT IT TAKES... YOU'RE GOING DOWN!
BAM
CHAPTER 7
STRONG ONE

ONE HOUR AGO
FSSH
POOF
HUH?
CRASH
IS THIS THE NEXT PLAYING FIELD?
NO ONE'S HERE YET.
POOF
WHA ...?
THUD

SQUISH
SO HEAVY!
SMACK
!
HOW DARE YOU CALL A LADY "HEAVY!"
THAT'S SO RUDE!
BY THE WAY...
WHY ARE YOU UNDER ME?
JUMP
HEY! *YOU* FELL ON *ME*!
?!
VWIP

TP
SMILE
A HANDSHAKE TO MAKE UP? ...
NO!
SWAP
PALM READING ...?
NO!
ROCK-PAPER-SCISSORS ...?
NO!
ASKING ME TO DANCE?!
IN YOUR DREAMS !!
YOU VIOLATED MY CIVIL RIGHTS.
PAY UP OR I'LL SUE!
LOOM
EEEP

SWP
THIS'LL COST YOU MORE THAN A CRACKER!
HEH...
THAT'S ALL I'VE GOT...
MUNCH
CRUNCH
WHAT'S YOUR NAME?
CRUNCH
MUNCH
SANSHIRO TAMON.
TAMON? THAT'S A WEIRD LAST NAME.
NICE TO MEET YOU, SANSHIRO.
I'M AKI HINO.
AKIHIRO?
THAT SOUNDS LIKE A BOY'S NAME.
AKI! HINO!
GRIND
DON'T BE SUCH A SMART ALECK!

YOU'RE DIFFERENT FROM THE OTHER PLAYERS.
REALLY?
THEY'RE ALL GLOOMY... THEY'RE SO SERIOUS ABOUT THIS GAME.
THEY'RE DESPERATE 'CAUSE THEY WANT TO GET THEIR WISH GRANTED.
GUESS I'M THE SAME THOUGH.
REALLY? WHAT ARE YOU WISHING FOR, AKI?
MONEY.
GRIP
WHAT AN EVIL FACE!!
I'D RATHER THEY WEREN'T SO STINGY GIVING US ONLY *ONE* WISH...
...BUT WITH ENOUGH MONEY YOU CAN *BUY* A LOT OF OTHER WISHES!
MONEY IS THE BEST!
REALLY?
ABSOLUTELY!

BUT STILL, IT DOES SEEM A BIT SUSPICIOUS ...
WHAT DOES ?
GOING TO THE TROUBLE OF CREATING THIS WORLD AND BRINGING KIDS OVER TO COMPETE AGAINST EACH OTHER...
WHAT DO THE MONSTERS GET OUT OF DOING ALL THIS?
AND I DON'T GET WHY THE GEKI FU MONSTERS COME OUT OF THE CARDS...
AND WHO ARE THE MYSTERIOUS PEOPLE WHO BROUGHT US HERE...?
THERE ARE TOO MANY THINGS WE DON'T KNOW.
SOMETHING STRANGE IS GOING ON HERE, BUT *WHAT*?
WHAT IF, AFTER WE GO THROUGH ALL THIS TROUBLE...
...IT'S ALL JUST A SETUP AND THERE'S NO WISH AT THE END?
NO
WHAT A COMPLETE WASTE OF TIME AND EFFORT!
NOOO!
DOESN'T MATTER TO ME... I'M JUST PLAYING FOR THE FUN OF IT.

WHAT?!
ARE YOU FOR REAL?!
HOW CAN YOU ENJOY PLAYING THESE GAMES?!
WOW! I KNEW YOU WERE A BIT WEIRD, BUT...
ARE YOU KIDDING? THIS IS THE MOST FUN I'VE EVER HAD!
GRIN
BUT THERE'S A RUMOR THAT WHEN YOU GET ELIMINATED AND GO BACK TO THE REAL WORLD...
...THEY ERASE ALL YOUR MEMORIES OF BACKWARDS JAPAN.
WHAT?!
FFT
BUT THEN IT'D BE LIKE THIS ADVENTURE NEVER EVEN HAPPENED!

THUD
GAH!
UGH...
FPT
FPT
TUP
THUD
OH!
LOOKS LIKE IT'S START-ING!
COUGH COUGH
HOLD ON! WAIT FOR ME...!
DASH
THUNK

WHOA!
GRAB
E-R-PANTSU
FWOOM
UMM... SORRY...
ZMM
FORGET YOU EVER SAW THAT!
HWAK

PRESENT TIME...
I KEEP TELLING YOU I'M SORRY!
IF APOLOGIES SETTLED EVERYTHING, THERE WOULDN'T BE A NEED FOR LAWYERS!!
GLARE
HAVE ANOTHER CRACKER...
I DON'T WANT IT!
SHUFFLE
I'M GOING TO PASS OUT THE GEKI FU BEFORE I EXPLAIN THE NEXT GAME!
HAHA HAHAHA
THIS TIME EACH OF YOU GETS ONLY ONE GEKI FU.
THE MONSTER IN EACH GEKI FU IS DIFFERENT!
SHUFFLE
NOW PICK A CARD, ANY CARD.
BUT ...
FWIP
CHOOSE WELL...
THE OUTCOME OF YOUR GAME WILL DEPEND ON IT!
GULP

SWIP
SWIP
SWIP
LET'S SEE, HOW ABOUT...
... THIS ONE?
SNATCH
HUH?!
SMIRK
GO AHEAD AND PICK FROM THE LEFT-OVERS!
HEE HEE HEE
WHAT'S WITH HER?!
THAT WAS THE CARD I WAS GONNA PICK...
?!
GLOW
SHEEN

OKAY!
DOES EVERYONE HAVE A GEKI FU?
GREAT!
THEN SUMMON YOUR MONSTER PARTNERS!
RING
COME ON! GIVE ME A STRONG ONE!
SWIP
EEEK!
COUGH COUGH
WHAT?!
WHAT'S WRONG WITH YOU?!
SQUEEZE
I...

DOOM
I HATE BUGS!
CLING
WHOA!
IT'S HUGE...
IS THAT YOUR GEKI FU?
EWW!
FLICK
SWIPE
SWIPE
CHITTER

OH!!

DOADO

DOOM
WOW! THEY ALL LOOK SO STRONG!
HERE I GO!
GIVE ME SOME-THING FIERCE!
SHIF

CHAPTER 8: A MONSTER'S FEELINGS

THIS IS SO COOL!
I GOT A GREAT MONSTER FOR MY PARTNER!
EVERYONE READY?
THE GAME IS ABOUT TO BEGIN.
HEY! WAIT A MINUTE!
I'VE GOT A B-BUG MONSTER!
SCREECH
I CAN'T TEAM UP WITH A BUG MONSTER!

FOR THIS ROUND, WE WILL PLAY "PILLAR KNOCK-DOWN!"
WHAT?
BUT WHERE'S THE PILLAR?
RIGHT HERE!
GRAB
RRIP!!
HE RIPPED A HOLE IN THE AIR!
FLAP

OM!!
?!

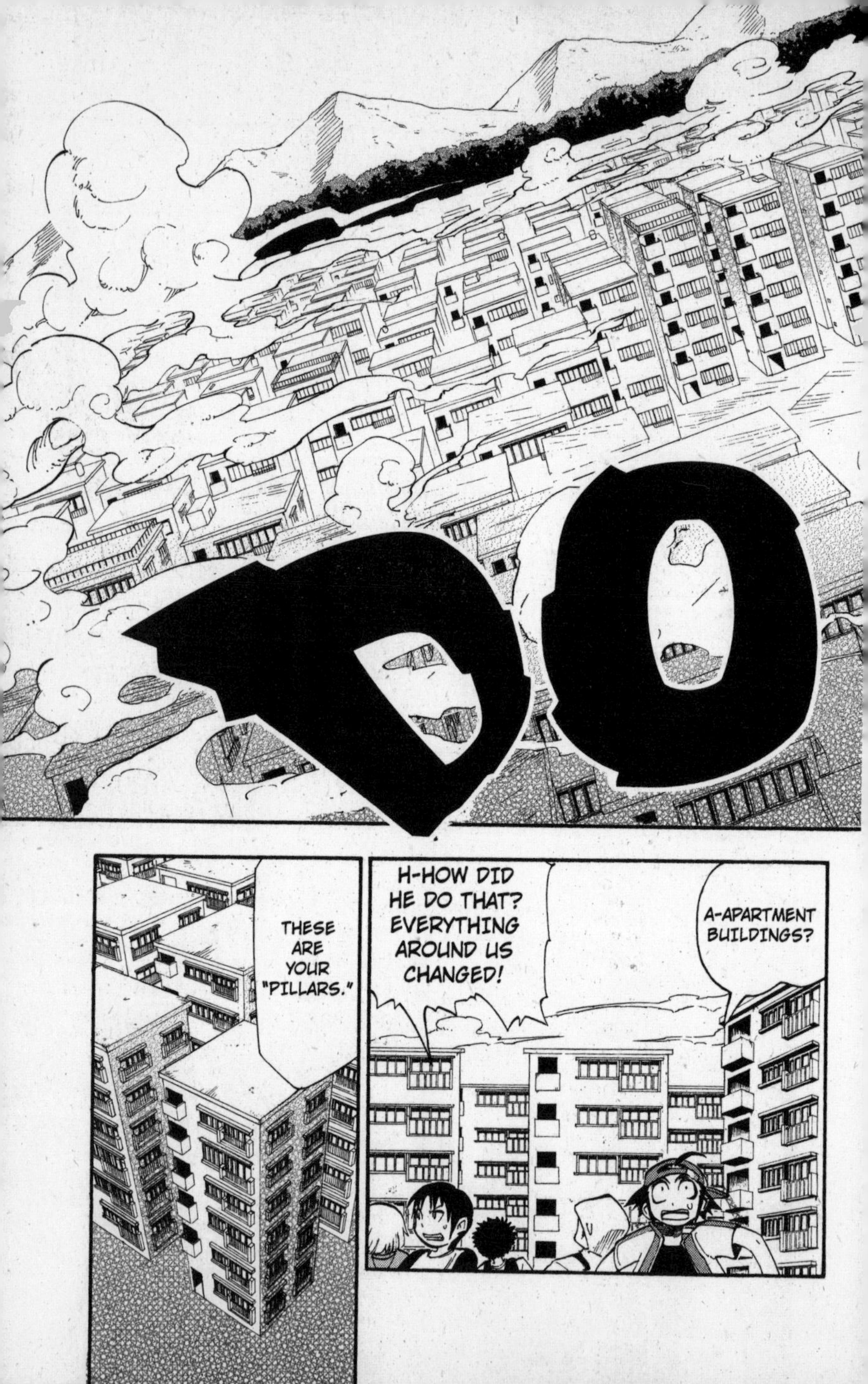
DO
A-APARTMENT BUILDINGS?
H-HOW DID HE DO THAT? EVERYTHING AROUND US CHANGED!
THESE ARE YOUR "PILLARS."

"JIN" MEANS "HUMAN" AND "KI" MEANS "OGRE."

"WAIRA" IS A MYTHICAL FROG CREATURE WITH SHARP CLAWS.

THAT'S "BU-GUMO"...
ITS QUALITIES ARE...
LET'S SEE...
"BU" MEANS "WARRIOR" AND "GUMO" (OR "KUMO") MEANS "SPIDER."
GURGLE
"MAIKA" SPRAYS A POWERFUL ACID THAT CAN MELT ANYTHING!
"MA" MEANS "EVIL" AND "IKA" MEANS "SQUID."
THAT ONE IS "USHI-TENGU."
USE ITS WIND POWERS WISELY!
FWAP
"USHI" MEANS "CATTLE" AND "TENGU" ARE MYTHICAL CROW CREATURES.
YEAH!
YOU THERE WITH THE RED HAT!!
VWIP
GEH HEH HEH
ALL THE MONSTERS LOOK SO STRONG THIS TIME!
"EN" MEANS "FLAME" AND "ZAN" MEANS "SLASH."
THAT'S WHAT YOU GET FOR THE WATER BLAST! ♥
...A SECRET! ♡
HMPH!
WHAT?!
ITS POWERS ARE...
THAT MONSTER'S NAME IS "ENZAN."
GROWWWL
SHF

THIS ROUND IS ALL ABOUT SPEED AND LUCK!!
HA HA HA HA
TWIRL
WAIT!
GOOD LUCK, EVERYBODY!!
RAAHH
ITS CLAWS ARE ITS WEAPONS, RIGHT?!
SLICE IT UP!
BOOM
SLASH

CRASH!!
WHOA!
AWW, TOO BAD... NO BELL RANG!
GET TO WORK, EVERYONE! THERE ARE PLENTY OF PILLARS TO KNOCK DOWN!
GO!
C'MON, LET'S DO IT!
SWSHH
SHK
SHK
SHK
CRUSH 'EM ALL TOGETHER!

SMASH
CLENCH
CRACK
BLURP
SIZZLE

THEY'RE DOING WELL! SUCH DESTRUCTION!
BOOM
CRASH
RUMBLE
SOMEONE'S GOING TO FIND A BELL SOON... I KNOW IT!
!
OOH! THERE'S ONE THAT HASN'T EVEN STARTED YET.
RRG
M-MOVE!!
SLUMP
AAGH!! THIS IS NO TIME FOR A NAP!
GO AWAY!
DON'T COME NEAR ME!
I HATE BUGS!
SCREECH?
RRM RRM

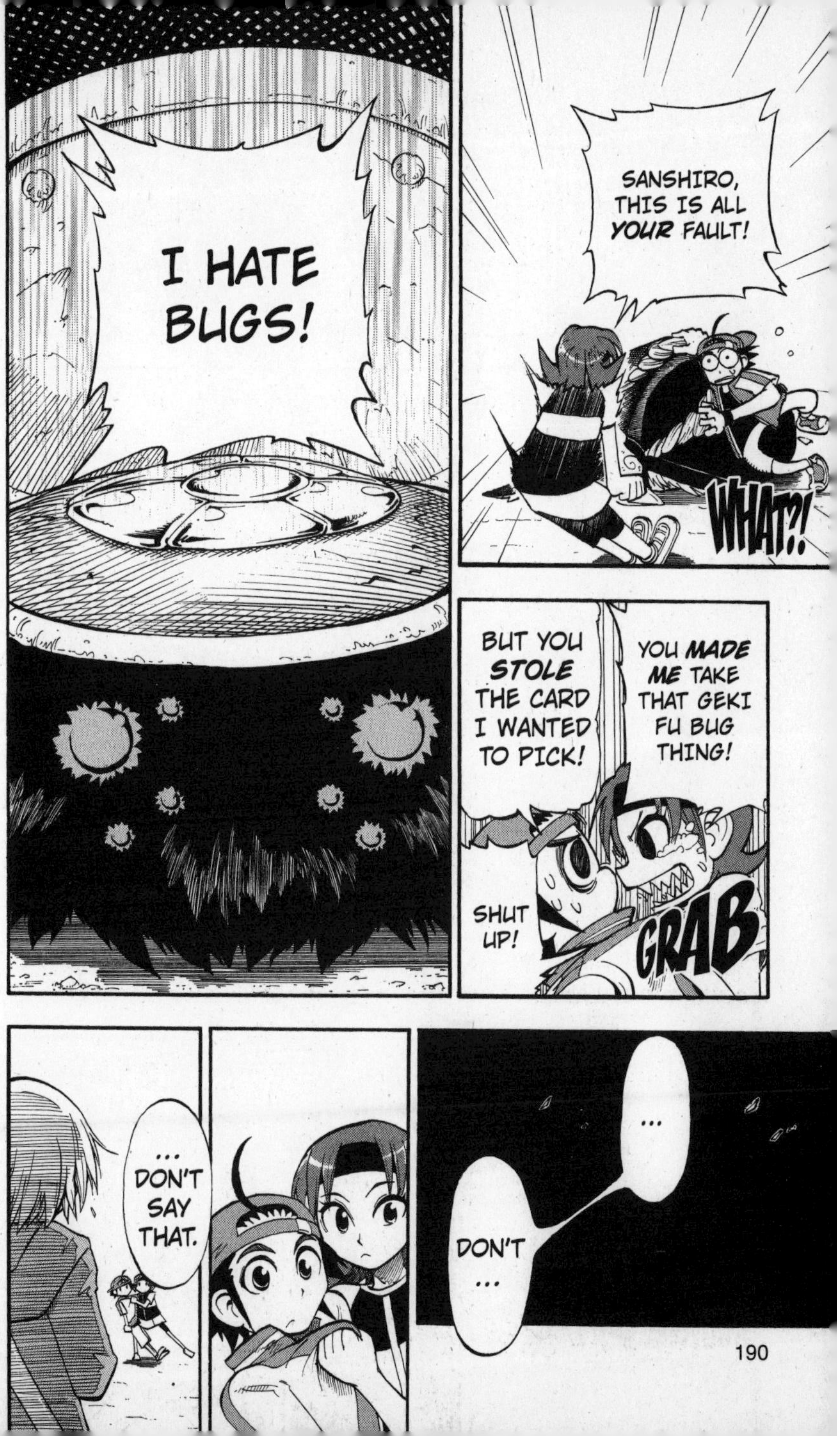
I HATE BUGS!
SANSHIRO, THIS IS ALL YOUR FAULT!
WHAT?!
YOU MADE ME TAKE THAT GEKI FU BUG THING!
BUT YOU STOLE THE CARD I WANTED TO PICK!
SHUT UP!
GRAB
... DON'T SAY THAT.
...
DON'T ...

GEKI FU MONSTERS ...
...HAVE FEELINGS ...
...TOO...
...
H-HEY!
TUP TUP TUP TUP
WHAT WAS THAT ABOUT ?
...
GEKI FU MONSTERS ...
...HAVE FEELINGS...

IS THAT ...?
IT CAN'T BE...
TUP TUP TUP
YES! I'M FIRST!
DING A LING
DING A LING
THERE'S THE BELL!
WE HAVE OUR FIRST WINNER!
DING A LING
CHITTER?
SHIVER
ULP!

PAT
...
I'M SORRY I SAID ALL THAT.
I NEVER GAVE YOU A FAIR CHANCE.
YOU WOULDN'T WANT TO HELP SOMEONE WHO HATES YOU.
I DIDN'T EVEN THINK ABOUT YOUR FEELINGS.
SHUNK
FLEX

FWOOM!
WHIRRRRRL
SMASH!

RUMBLE
WOW ...
WOOOO
YOU'RE AMAZING, BUGUMO!!
HUG
THANK YOU FOR YOUR HELP!
CHITTER
YOU'RE SO POWERFUL! THIS IS AWESOME!
KNOCK THEM ALL DOWN!!
BOING
BOING
CRASH
CRUMBLE
KEEP IT UP, BUGUMO!
HEE HEE.

The Real Game Guide

The games that Sanshiro must clear in the preliminary rounds are based on actual games in Japan. Some may be familiar and some may be completely foreign to you. But since this all takes place in Backwards Japan, not everything is the way it should be!

Ogre Tag (鬼ごっこ: Oni Gokko)

The game of tag in Japanese is literally called "playing ogre" (*oni gokko*). The person that is "it" is called the "ogre" (*oni*). So when Sanshiro and the other players are playing Ogre Tag, they're really playing with an ogre!

Regular tag in Japan follows the same rules as in America. But in Backwards Japan, the players are trying to touch the ogre instead of running away from it like you would in a real game of tag.

Shadow Stepping (影踏み: Kage Fumi)

Shadow Stepping is just like the game of tag, except that instead of touching the person, whoever is "it" has to step on their shadow to catch them. In this Backwards Japan version of the game, the players can only move by staying in the shadows of Suijin fish that are pursuing them.

Pillar Knockdown (棒倒し: Bô Taoshi)

In Japanese, *bô* means "pillar," which will usually be a stick or a long pole depending on the way this game is played. There are two different ways that this game is played in Japan.

The more simple playground game is where the players build a mound in the sandbox and place a stick in the top. The players take turns removing a scoop of sand from the mound without making the stick fall. Whoever makes the stick fall is the loser. But in Backwards Japan, the winner is the one who knocks down the pillar (or, in this case, an apartment building) and finds the hidden bell inside.

The more difficult version is usually played at Sports Day festivals at school. In this game, teams (or classes) each have their own pillar. The object of the game is to knock down other teams' pillars while defending your own. Once a pillar has fallen over (or just partially fallen over), that team is out.

Backwards Game
BAKÉGYAMON
SHORT COMIC
ALL RIGHT! MAKE CLONES OF YOURSELF, DORO-KOZO!
SCURRY
SCURRY
SCURRY
PANT
PANT
PANT
PANT
PANT
PANT
THEY'RE STARTING TO LOOK BAD...
SQUASH